No Bunnies Here!

By **Tammi Sauer**

Illustrated by **Ross Burach**

WELCOME TO
Bunnyville
Land of a
THOUSAND
BUNNIES!

BUNNYVILLE
HOPPY DAY
PARADE

Today!

Doubleday Books for Young Readers

Oh!

Hello there, Wolf. My, uh, what big teeth you have.

You look—*gulp*—hungry.

Too bad there's nothing yummy here. Goodbye.

That?

Uh, that is
not a bunny.

Clearly, it's a lamp.

Heh. There are certainly lots of interesting things around this place.

Grass. That clump of dirt. More grass. But a bunny?

Nope. There are no bunnies here.

Well! Would you look at what the wind blew our way!

Have you ever seen such a perfect pair of . . .

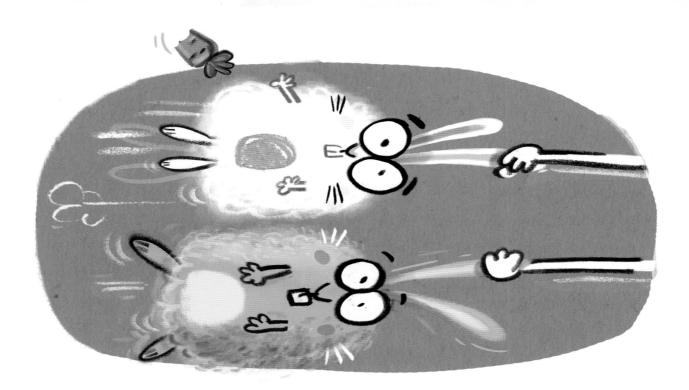

SQUISHY PILLOWS?

I think I'll cozy up right here and take a nap. Nighty-night!

Oh, dear. That is definitely *not* a bunny parade.
You must be confused, Wolf.
Perhaps you just need to relax.
I know! Take a vacation!
I hear Antarctica is lovely this time of year.
Please give my regards to the penguins.

Bon voyage!
Au revoir!

Now would a bunny
speak French?
I think not.

THEN **WHY** ARE YOU TRYING SO HARD TO **FIND A BUNNY?**

Wait, Wolf. Please stay.
But there's something
you should know:

In this place,
you won't find one
single friend. . . .

You'll find a whole bunny bunch!

There are *lots* of bunnies here.